For Neil, who is *never* grumpy . . . .
~ S. J.

For Ronald and Peggy—I've never known
them to have a grumpy day, ever!
~ A. E.

tiger tales
5 River Road, Suite 128, Wilton, CT 06897
Published in the United States 2016
Originally published in Great Britain 2016
by Little Tiger Press
Text copyright © 2016 Stella J. Jones
Illustrations copyright © 2016 Alison Edgson
ISBN-13: 978-1-68010-012-9
ISBN-10: 1-68010-012-2
Printed in China
LTP/1400/1249/0915

10 9 8 7 6 5 4 3 2 1

For more insight and activities,
visit us at www.tigertalesbooks.com

The VERY Grumpy Day

by Stella J. Jones

Illustrated by Alison Edgson

tiger tales

"What a perfect day!" smiled Mouse, looking out at the sunshine.

And goodness, he was right! The birds trilled sweetly, and the bees buzzed merrily.

"I'll take one of these cupcakes to Bear," Mouse said. "He loves a sweet treat."

Mouse tappity-tap-tapped
on Bear's front door. But
he didn't know that Bear
had just left . . .

BEAR

. . . in a *very* bad mood.

"Oh, hmph!" grumped Bear.

"These boots are just TOO BIG!"

Bear stomped along so heavily that the ground shivered and shook beneath his feet.

STOMP!

STOMP!   STOMP!

"**Hey!**" cried Mole angrily, popping up from his mole hole. "Your stomping has made my tunnel collapse. I have to start all over again!"

He flung down his shovel and had just disappeared into his hole when . . .

... "**Aaaaahhhhhhh!**"

Hedgehog tripped over the shovel
with a bump.

"Who left THAT there?" he cried.

He roly-polied across
the clearing . . .

. . . straight into Fox's bottom.

"OOOOOOOOOWWWWWW!" Fox yelped.

"Watch where you're poking your
prickles, Hedgehog!" Fox jumped
up and his bag flew high
into the air.

The groceries tumbled out . . .

. . . and plopped all over the squirrel family!

SPLAT went the bag of flour!

SPLOSH went the milk!

And **SMASH** went the eggs all over the baby squirrels!

"Be quiet down there!"
screeched Daddy Owl.
"You'll wake my chicks!"

Now everyone was in a **BIG BAD** mood.

QUARREL!

Up above, the sky turned dark.
A roll of thunder shook the woods,
and the rain began to fall.

"Oh, no!" grumped Bear. "There's a hole in my umbrella and my ears are getting wet."

Bear's bad mood lasted all the way home. Then suddenly, he spotted something.

"It's a present! For me!"
Bear picked it up and read
the note. "Oh, how nice!"
he sniffed.

And for the very first time
that day, Bear smiled.

As Bear munched happily on his cupcake, the sky cleared, and the flowers bobbed in the breeze.

"Mole would love these flowers," said Bear. "I'll take them over to him to apologize for stomping on his tunnel."

"I'm sorry, Mole," said Bear,
giving the flowers to his friend.
"That's okay," said Mole.
And for the first time that
day, Mole smiled, too.

"I should say I'm sorry to Hedgehog
for leaving my shovel in his way,"
said Mole. He trotted over to
his friend's house and gave
Hedgehog a huge hug.

The smiles and happiness spread like rays of spring sunshine all through the afternoon.

When Mouse looked out his window,
the entire woods were ringing with
birdsong and laughter.

"Such a perfect day," he beamed,
racing out to join his friends.

And it was!